# When We Grow Up

Copyright © Cawanna King, 2020. All Rights Reserved.

Published in Suitland Maryland, United States.

No part of this book may be reproduced in any form or by any electronic or mechanical means, including information storage and retrieval systems, without permission in writing from the publisher, except by a reviewer who may quote brief passages in a review.
First edition, August 2020

ISBN 978-1-7353856-2-4: Hardcover
ISBN 978-1-7353856-0-0: Paperback
ISBN 978-1-7353856-1-7: Ebook
Library of Congress Control Number: 2020912903

Front Cover Image by Tashema Davis
Book Design by Molo Global Publishing

www.whenwegrowup.com

This book is dedicated to my mother, Aubrey Jean King, and my grandmother, Nellie Shelton King. May they both rest in peace.

When I grow up, I'll make a million bucks, like the movie stars on tv.

In that case, I'll be twirling on stage. The world will love to see "The Great Monique" dance.

And I'll fly "LaShundria Air" to all of your shows in the South of France.

We can hit all the fashion runways. We'll wear pretty clothes and high heel shoes.

Or I could sit behind a great big desk and report the evening news.

Maybe I could be an artist. Mommy says my paintings are the best!

I bet if I were a detective, I'd make all those bad guys confess.

I'll try out for the Olympics. You can cheer as I go for the gold.

And I can say, "Order in the court!" as I sit on a bench in my long black robe.

When it's time to choose a new president, maybe I'll throw my hat in the ring.

And I can walk around waving signs that say "Vote for LaShundria King."

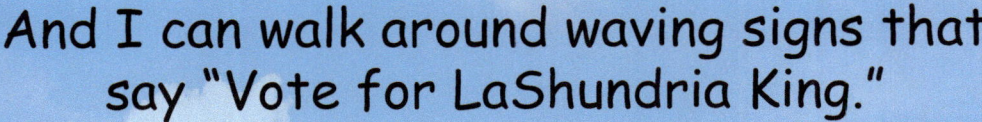

What if I was the driver of a big yellow bus? I'd drive as careful as can be.

The world could always use more good teachers, maybe I could be one.

I'll teach my whole class to read and say stuff like "Stay in your seats!" or "Spit out your gum!"

I would love to feed the homeless. I'm sure it's hard living on the streets.

We could be mediators like mommy. Wouldn't that be great?

We'll say "Don't start fighting when you disagree. We'll be there to mediate."

I can run my own science lab. I'd do a great job, that's for sure.

So when someone gets sick and nothing seems to work, I could help find a cure.

I could design buildings, like an architect. You know mommy always says I'm a really smart girl.

We could even start our own business. We'll plan the best parties, yep, that's what we'll do.

We'd have all kinds of fun stuff, like popcorn, cotton candy and snow cones too.

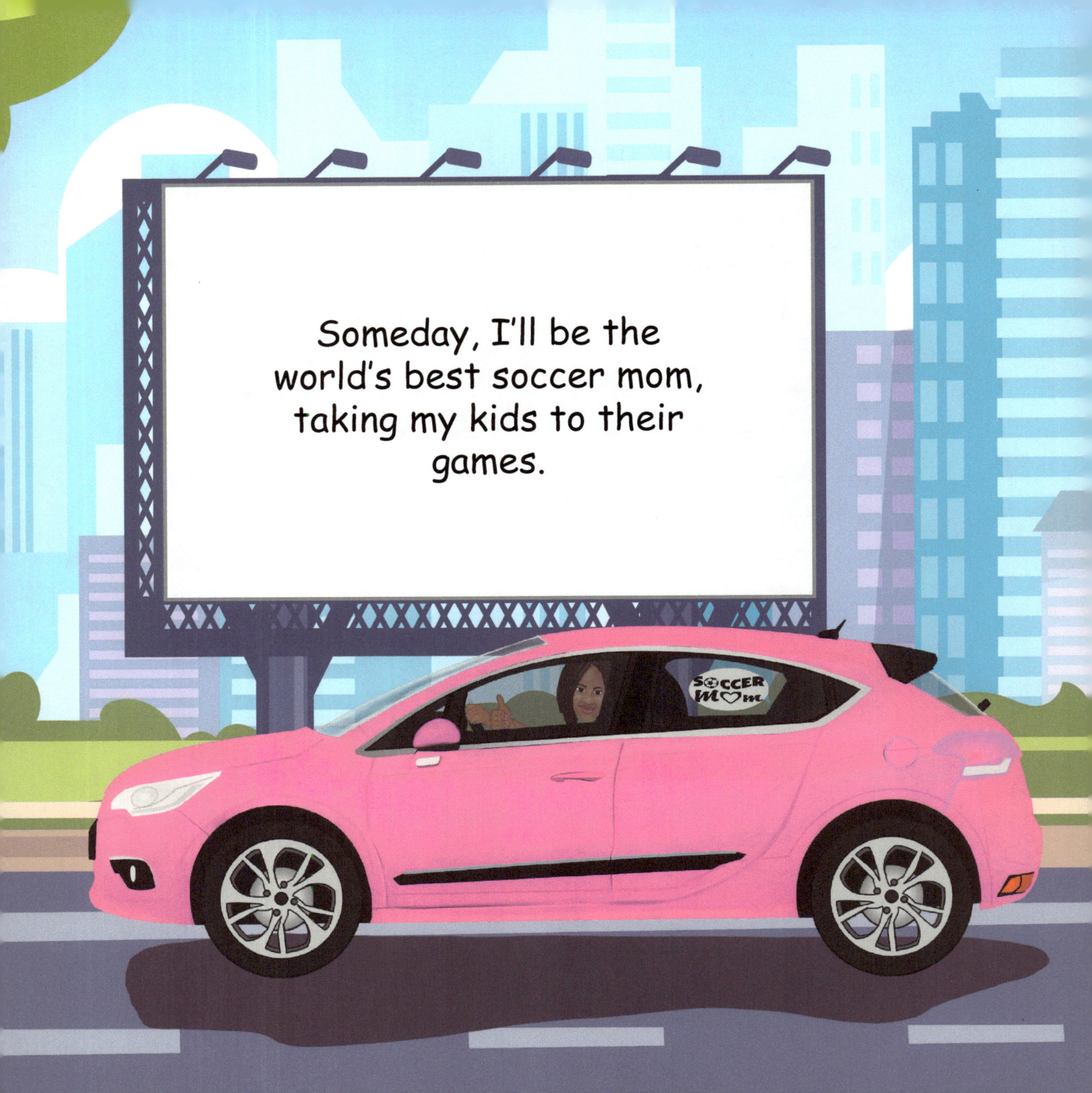

I'll be in the stands yelling "Goal!" and screaming out their names.

It's never too early to do what you love. You have the power to decide.

# ACKNOWLEDGEMENTS

First and foremost, I'd like to thank God for placing this book in my head and these thoughts in my heart.

Thank you to my daughters, Lashundria and Monique, for being my inspiration. I pray that you both spend your lives doing the things that bring you joy and doing the work that feeds your souls.

Thank you to my husband, Charles Mack, for supporting all my wacky dreams, like that one time I wanted to be a housewife and stay-at-home mom.

Thank you to my cousin, Naomi Connor. It was reading your first book that gave me the courage to write my own. I appreciate your guidance and encouragement.

Thank you to Tashema Davis, my illustrator, for bringing my vision to life. I appreciate your patience and enthusiasm with this project.

Last, but certainly not least, I'd like to thank my friend and mentor, Tracee Ford, for convincing me to finally complete this labor of love, and to share it with the world.

Cawanna King is a wife, mother, and serial community volunteer. The Texas native is a longtime resident of Prince George's County, Maryland, where she is a certified mediator and a trained conflict coach.

The first-time author is married to Charles Mack, a retiree and avid bowler. Her hobbies include spoiling her grand puppy, Diamond, and listening to her daughters', LaShundria and Monique's, coming of age tales and often humorous misadventures.

Tashema Davis is an Indiana-based artist. While she studied Interior design and Art Education, Tashema was drawn toward the fascinating world of illustration. After having taught high school art for several years, Tashema now enjoys illustrating children's books during her down time. The illustrations for 'When We Grow Up...!' were created using mainly Procreate.

Tashema lives in Marion, Indiana, with her husband and their two daughters.

www.tnicole.com

www.whenwegrowup.com